Nobody's Perfect, Not Even My Mother

Norma Simon

Pictures by Dora Leder

ALBERT WHITMAN & COMPANY, MORTON GROVE, ILLINOIS

For Ed, Steffi, Wendy, and Jon,
with love and gratitude.

Library of Congress Cataloging-in-Publication Data

Simon, Norma.
   Nobody's perfect, not even my mother.

   (Concept books/level 1)
   Summary: A young child learns that nobody's perfect,
yet people can be wonderful just the same.
      I. Leder, Dora.   II. Title.
PZ7.S6053No   [E]   81-520
ISBN 0-8075-5707-2   AACR1

A Note About This Book

We try and try, all of our lives, to do things well because we need to please ourselves as much as we need to please others.

We try and we succeed. We try and we fail. We try again.

Young children, especially, crave the recognition, encouragement, and praise which reward them for each new achievement. And when they fail in some way, they are their own severest critics. They need tolerant and comforting reassurance that perfection is not always possible in all things, even for those powerful and competent beings, their parents and teachers.

The gentle reminders and humor in this book can stimulate children and grownups to explore and discuss this basic concept.

NORMA SIMON

Nobody's perfect.
That's what *I* say.

I'm not perfect,
but I get some things
exactly right.

I get every piece in place with my puzzles.

I know I'm not perfect,

but I'm pretty good

at somersaults.

See?

I take pretty good pictures,

but not perfect.

Grandma likes them, anyway.

When I really try
to do something right,

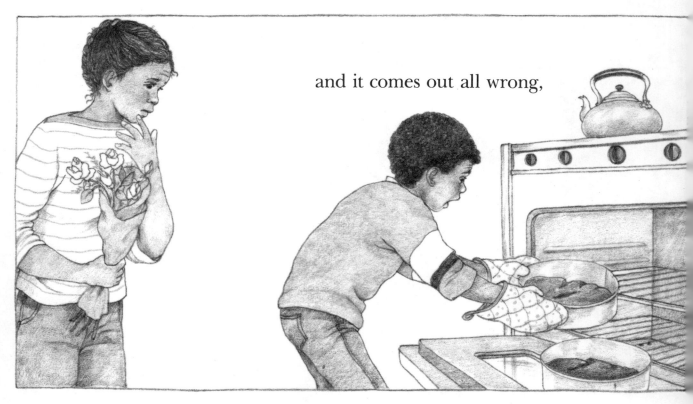

and it comes out all wrong,

I feel awful. Just awful!

I get angry at myself!

I get angry at my cat!

I want to get it right. My sister helps me.

Well, it's not perfect, but Mom likes it.

My mother's perfect with machines.
She works on new cars.

She knows how to make them just right.
But she's not perfect about everything.

She tries to stop smoking.
Smoking's bad for her.

She tries, but she says
it's hard to stop.

My father's perfect with bricks—
brick chimneys, brick walls, brick houses.

Every brick in place,
      every brick just right.

But he's not perfect when he gets mad.
Then he yells at us a lot.
He scares me when he does that.

He says he's going to try to stop.
I hope he can.
I really hope he can.

Grandpa says, "Nobody's perfect, especially me.
Lots of new things to learn all the time."

He practices his guitar every night.
He plays a few songs,
        but he's sure not perfect.

Grandma always tells me
    she doesn't know everything.
And she looks up lots of things
    about dinosaurs and turtles, about
    vegetables, and about her work.
She's a doctor for animals.
She has lots of books to help her.

My puppy is learning.
He's growing up,
            but he's not perfect.
I hate it when Mom yells at him.

My kitten scratches the new chair.
She scratches me, too.

I like her,
but kittens are *not* perfect!
No way!

Even teachers aren't perfect.
Know what ours did?

She left her keys inside her house.
She had to climb in the window.

Everyone wants to be perfect
at something—

making things out of wood—

painting horses—

counting money.

I'm not perfect in English
the way I am in Vietnamese.

But I'm learning.
We're all learning.

Every day my dad and I practice ball.
Every day we practice hard.

Today I got it.
I got it right!
I got it just right!

You're good at some things—
I'm good at some things.

Everyone's good at some things.

Billings County Public School Dist. No. 1
Box 307
Medora, North Dakota 58645

But nobody's perfect!